ONE FINE DAY

ONE FINE DAY
by Nonny Hogrogian

Aladdin Paperbacks

Aladdin Paperbacks. An imprint of Simon & Schuster Children's Publishing Division, 1230 Avenue of the Americas, New York, NY 10020. Copyright © 1971 by Nonny Hogrogian. All rights reserved including the right of reproduction in whole or in part in any form. Library of Congress catalog card number: 75-119834. First Aladdin Paperbacks edition, 1986. Also available in a hardcover edition from Simon & Schuster Books for Young Readers. Printed in the United States of America.   ISBN 0-02-043620-3

20   19   18   17   16   15

For Liza and Zacky

One fine day

a fox traveled through a great forest.

When he reached the other side he was very thirsty.

He saw a pail of milk that an old woman had set down
while she gathered wood for her fire. Before she noticed the fox,
he had lapped up most of the milk.

The woman became so angry that she grabbed her knife and chopped off his tail, and the fox began to cry.

"Please, old woman, give me back my tail. Sew it in place or all my friends will laugh at me."

"Give me back my milk," she said, "and I'll give you back your tail."

So the fox dried his tears and went to find a cow.

"Dear cow," he begged, "please give me some milk so I can give it to the old woman so she will sew my tail in place."

The cow replied, "I'll give you some milk if you bring me some grass."

The fox called to the field, "Oh beautiful field, give me some grass.
I'll take it to the cow and she'll give me some milk. Then
I'll take the milk to the old woman so she will sew my tail in place
and I can return to my friends."

The field called back, "Bring me some water."

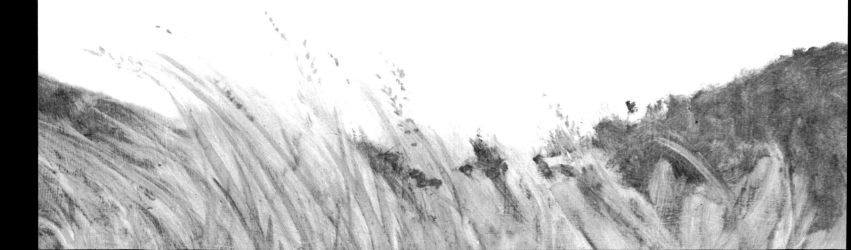

The fox ran to the stream and begged for some water,
and the stream answered, "Bring me a jug."

The fox found a fair maiden. "Sweet maiden," he said,
"please give me your jug so I can fetch some water to give the field
to get some grass to feed the cow to get some milk to give
the old woman to sew my tail in place so I can return to my friends."

The maiden smiled. "If you find a blue bead for me," she said,
"I will give you my jug."

So the fox found a peddler and said, " There is a pretty maiden
down the road and if you give me one blue bead for her she'll be
pleased with you and pleased with me. Then she'll give me her jug
so I can fetch some water to give the field to get some grass
to feed the cow to get some milk to give the old woman
to sew my tail in place."

But the peddler was not taken in by the promise of a pretty smile
or the cleverness of the fox and he replied, "Pay me an egg
and I'll give you a bead."

The fox went off and found a hen.

"Hen, dear hen, please give me an egg to give to the peddler
in payment for the bead to get the jug to fetch the water
to give the field to get some grass to feed the cow to get the milk
that I must give the old woman in return for my tail."

The hen clucked. "I'll trade you an egg for some grain."

The fox was getting desperate, and when he found the miller
he began to cry.

"Oh kind miller, please give me a little grain. I have to trade it
for the egg to pay the peddler to get the blue bead to give the maiden
in return for her jug to fetch the water to give the field
to get the grass to feed the cow to get the milk to give the old woman
so she'll sew my tail in place, or all my friends will laugh at me."

The miller was a good man and felt sorry for the fox.

So he gave him the grain to give to the hen to get the egg

to pay the peddler to get the bead

to give the maiden to get the jug to fetch the water

to give the field to get the grass to feed the cow

to get the milk to give the old woman to get his tail back.

The fox returned to the old woman and gave her the milk.

Then she carefully sewed his tail in place,

and off he ran to join his friends on the other side of the forest.